Meanwhile

Kayleigh Hughes

All characters, events, and places, are entirely fictitious. Any similarities to actual people, living or deceased, places, or events, are coincidental. All rights served. No part of this publication may be reproduced or transmitted in any form or by any means, without permission from the author.

Copyright © 2021 Kayleigh Hughes

All rights reserved.

For Mrs. Reilly, and my beloved dad, without whom, my passion for writing would not exist.

Thanks to Sonia, for your invaluable help with some of the finer details.

'An impressive beginning that does not always venture into obvious places. It packs a lot for its relatively short length. Highly recommended.'

"Meanwhile..." defies attempts to pin it down from the very beginning as it deftly threads the needles of several genres at once.'

'The relevance of the main characters situation is so on point in today's society. That moment you realize what's going on, it hits you like a ton of bricks...in a good way.'

CONTENTS

One 1

Two 6

Three 9

Four 15

Five 17

Six 32

Seven 38

Eight 55

Nine 59

Ten 65

Eleven 68

Twelve 88

Thirteen 92

Fourteen 99

BOOK I

One

He was almost there. Nine minutes. Samuel would make it. He'd need to, anyway, for Joan's sake. And professionalism. But mainly Joan. Samuel didn't want a repeat of last Tuesday. Conducting his work in the community centre, and not in the comfort of his own home. Bloody hell, why, you bastard. For his clients' sake, he supposed. And there was still Alesha's session on Thursday to reschedule. If there was anything Samuel was certain of this week, it was his time with his supervisor Rachel. Marvellous lady, she was. As Samuel skimmed through the busy crowd, he spied his watch - just time to take a slash. Two minutes, maybe three, then straight to the station. Food would just have to wait. Samuel's leather case swung around in his sweaty grip. Curse this bastard heatwave, curse the saturated - and only clean - shirt pasted to him. His sticky dark hair bobbed up and down on his forehead as he picked up speed.

Oh, at last. Samuel hurried through the entrance, heading straight for the men's. Approaching the long steel urinal, he wheezed slightly as his heart thumped in his chest. Forty-two, and probably couldn't walk a marathon, let alone run one, even as a lanky six footer. Bit too keen on the subs, so Harriet reckoned. His face was probably as pink as the toilet walls. Samuel placed down his case, and at last relieved himself. Lovely and cool was that air conditioning, too. He glanced at his watch - seven minutes. He wouldn't-

Sod it.

Samuel rushed to the sink, and splashed water over his hands. He bound out of the toilet, down the path, and towards the station, huffing and puffing. Ticket - where was his -

got it! The gate was seconds away. Samuel flashed his ticket at the staff member, and hurried to the platform. Joan would understand if he was late, wouldn't she? He'd call her on the journey there. Samuel stepped onto the train, with...four minutes to spare. The carriage was virtually empty, until the next stop, anyway. He collapsed into the nearest seat, exhaling a huge sigh. He'd have to take his blood pressure when he returned home - or even get Harriet to do it in the morning, when she had finished her shift in the ICU. He just needed to check his notes for Joan, just to...

Shit.

His case. Still in the-

Samuel bolted off the train, and back into the station. He had to - Joan. Shit, shit, shit. Samuel exclaimed a frantic flurry of 'sorry's, as he bumped into other people passing by. The case - grab the case, then phone Joan.

The toilet door swung open, and Samuel stumbled through. He stopped, seeing a woman in a cleaner uniform crouched towards the case. Which was open, with some of its content scattered on the floor. The woman looked about his age, maybe older, judging from the greying crop of hair, and slightly sagging skin. A little plump, but probably fit enough, given the nature of her job.

'I take it this is yours?'

And on forty a day, by the sounds of it.

Samuel approached the case, tidying up the scattered sheets. The woman stepped away. The train. Too late. He'd have to phone Joan while he waited for the next one. She'd understand, she wasn't a tyrant or pain in the arse, or anything. He'd hate to let her down. Samuel clicked his case shut, and stood upright. Thirty minutes, plenty of time. He headed for the door, and pull-

It didn't budge.

Samuel turned.

The woman was pointing a gun at him.

Two

'That's not how this works, Mr Moylan.'

Peter Moylan sat, holding a half empty glass of gin and tonic. He rubbed at his baggy eyes, scratching at his white beard. A fine suite in this fine house of his, if Samuel didn't say so himself. Moylan tapped his fingers on his glass, occasionally meeting Samuel's gaze.

'What can you tell me, Samuel? I am Joan's family, after all.'

People just didn't seem to understand how this profession worked, sometimes. For the best part of the last thirty minutes, Moylan had been - how could Samuel put it...nagging like a gossiping grandmother. What had Joan told her brother?

'And please,' Peter continued. 'I insist, call me Peter, I'm not a doctor. She hasn't been thinking of suicide, has she?'

Samuel shook his head.

'I'm only here because of her spell during our last session, and just wanted to make sure she got home okay.'

Moylan took a swig, nodding, as though understanding, but Samuel didn't think he did.

'Does that breach shrink boundaries, or confidentiality, or whatever it is?'

'I'm a therapist, Mr Moylan,' Samuel replied. 'I don't-'

'Is it depression?'

Samuel sighed.

'You will have to talk to Joan about this, yourself. I cannot divulge confidential information, with certain exceptions.'

The average person would have read Moylan's expression as mere curiosity, but unfortunately Samuel knew better.

'If Joan is at risk of harming herself or anyone else,' Samuel continued. 'The possibility of sexual abuse, whether at present or in childhood. Or if she is involved in criminal or terrorist activity.'

Moylan took another sip, and rubbed the back of his neck.

'Tell me that again, only like a human.'

Three

All at once, Samuel Manson had forgotten about everything. The train. Joan. Harriet. His case. Even the fact that he hadn't eaten in six hours. His eyes were trained on the barrel of the gun currently pointed at him. Then the woman. Her blank expression.

'You'll have to do, I suppose.'

Samuel didn't move. Didn't speak.

'You're a therapist. Not the right one, but a therapist.'

His eyes wouldn't budge. They couldn't. Gradually, Samuel raised his hands - that was the correct thing to do, wasn't it? The woman nodded, motioning for him to move against and face the wall. Samuel complied. His lack of response, was it stemming from the nature of his job - to listen; to not judge; to do whatever the hell this woman said? He could at least try convincing himself of it, anyway. Samuel's eyes darted around the cold wall.

'What if...someone else...needs...in here?'

The woman pulled him around to face her. She shrugged.

Bloody hell...great first words there, Samuel. Not as if his life was on the line, was it? The woman's shrug said only one thing: not her cock-a-doodling problem.

'What do you need?'

The woman placed her gun down on the sink. From her pocket, she produced a cable tie, and secured his wrist to the pipes beside the sink.

'Where's your phone?'

With his free hand, Samuel fumbled about in his pocket, then passed his mobile to the woman.

'I need to make a call,' he said quickly.

It was ultimately in vain, as Samuel guessed his chances of doing such to be not even remote. Harriet. Joan. Were they as worried as he was? Would Joan be annoyed? Upset at yet another delay? As forgiving as Harriet had had no business being in their twenty year marriage? The woman looked at him.

'Not the police,' Samuel continued. 'My client. M-My wife. They'll be-'

The phone slipped into the woman's pocket. Pathetic, that was pathetic, Samuel cursed into himself. The woman lifted the gun, creasing her forehead. The blankness had not changed.

'In Andrew McNally's "professional opinion"...help.'

'What?'

'You asked what I need,' the woman continued. 'Well-'

'Let me call my client. Please. I have a duty of care. Do you understand that?'

She shot up, and began to pace. She stopped, staring Samuel dead in the eyes.

'Loud and clear,' she said curtly, though Samuel sensed it was quite the opposite. 'Do *you* understand that isn't going to happen, of course?'

Samuel nodded. The woman's expression softened, but her bitter tone remained, though Samuel detected what seemed like an underlying panic.

'I'm Caroline Louise Cleaver,' she barked like a drill sergeant. 'A name you are not going to forget. Is that understood?'

Samuel nodded. 'Of course.'

He glanced over at his case, then at Caroline.

'I guess you already know my name's Samuel.'

'Hm.'

For several moments, Samuel surveyed the woman. The gun in her hand, which he rather doubted was just for show.

'So...what's this all about, Caroline? What's brought this on?'

Caroline removed Samuel's phone from her pocket, holding it out to him. He had anticipated some sort of answer, yes, but not the one that followed.

'Tell your wife and Joan there's been a holdup, and that the evening news will explain everything.'

'What-'.

BANG! BANG!

Samuel flinched, looking at Caroline as she lowered the gun, and then at the two bullet holes piercing the toilet door. Then froze at the screams sounding from the other side.

Four

Oh, I quite insist, it won't be on my conscience, Muriel.'

Moylan stood against the sink, eyeing the younger Muriel Pollock's backside as she slid paper into the printer.

'Bipolar, that's what you reckon it is?'

It was almost as alluring as her hazel eyes. Or those golden locks, just the ideal length for him to ruffle. That trendy figure he'd play like a pinball machine.

'Reckoning is out of the question, my dear. What time is your date tonight?'

Muriel smiled, as the photocopier began flashing and whirring.

'About seven,' she replied, reaching for more paper. 'Fancy restaurant too. Nicest meal I'll have had in a while.'

And spoil that slender figure, with spaghetti, or steak pie, or some other abomination? Dear, oh, dear. A chicken salad would surely suffice. Moylan returned the smile, eyes wandering to the woman's breasts.

'Do tell me how it goes, on Monday, won't you?'

The photocopier stopped, and Muriel removed the pages, clearing her throat.

'Of course.'

Five

Samuel listened to the commotion on the other side. People clamouring for the police. Caroline gripped her gun.

'I'm not the best shot,' she said, the panic gradually creeping into her voice. 'That was probably into thin air.'

'Caroline, if it's me you want to talk to, why did you do that? You've practically pissed away your exit options.'

Caroline heaved out a sigh, and passed Samuel his phone.

'Call them, tell them what I originally told you to.'

Samuel looked at her.

'Because I want to talk to the police.'

As he dialled, a burning question lurked in his mind.

'Who exactly is Andrew McNally, Caroline?'

Samuel knew he wouldn't get an answer, watching Caroline aim her gun at him. He just hoped either Harriet or Joan picked up. Samuel listened to the ringing on the other end. Pick up, Harriet, come on. The outside world had likely caught wind of this incident by now. The station cordoned off - on lockdown. Swamped with police - armed forces too, no doubt. Journalists, news crew - the whole bloody works, fighting to the teeth for the best front page. All because he had accidentally forgotten his case, because his time management was as fucked as his nerves. Harriet was in the hospital, she was bound to have-'

'Samuel? What is it, what's-'

Thank bloody Christ.

'Harriet,' Samuel began, his voice sharp and tense. 'Harriet, are you able to see the news, at all?'

'Yeah, we've got it on - Jesus, Samuel, are you all right?'

He didn't know who was more worried.

'At the moment, yes - but Harriet, listen, have they reported any casualties?'

'Do you not-'

'Not from inside the toilet.'

He drew in sharp breaths at the agonising pause on Harriet's end.

'Oh God, Samuel, are you serious?'

'Yes,' he replied. 'But please, don't panic, my love. Don't panic.'

He momentarily shut his eyes, wishing for this all to be over. For his wife's sake. For

Joan's sake. There'd be little point in calling her now, as she'd probably found out from the news about whatever the hell all this was. What would he tell her, anyway? Leaving both Harriet and his client Joan in distress about all this was not what he wanted on his conscience, but unfortunately already was. Whatever the woman opposite him wanted, he wished it would just happen. Whatever this Andrew McNally meant to her, he wished she would just tell him.

A voice called from the other side of the door.

'Everyone please clear this area - this is a major incident! Clear this area now, thank you!'

Samuel watched as Caroline impatiently motioned her gun at him.

'Harriet, I'm sorry, I'm going to have to go.'

'*I love you.*'

'Love you, too,' he said, and hung up.

Knock, knock.

Samuel looked as Caroline moved towards the door, her gun lowered.

'My name is Owen Buckley, I'm the Police Negotiator. Who am I speaking to?'

Long pause.

'Caroline.'

Samuel noted the derision in her tone.

'Okay,' Buckley replied. 'is there anyone else with you in the toilet, Caroline?'

She turned to Samuel, motioning to the door.

'Samuel!'

Surely Buckley would have been able to hear a second voice - perhaps he was just making sure?

'Okay, Caroline and Samuel,' Buckley continued. 'I just want to-'

'I didn't mean to hurt anyone,' Caroline blurted out. 'If I did.'

'We do have one casualty, yes. But we'd preferably like there not to be any more by the end of this, okay?'

Samuel looked at Caroline, slight annoyance seeming to have manifest.

'Why'd you do it in the first place, then, Caroline?'

Caroline took a step back, a little startled by the frustrated tone. She gazed at the floor.

'I don't know.'

It was quiet, almost inaudible.

'Is that okay, Caroline?'

Their heads cocked to Buckley's voice.

'What?' Caroline replied.

'For there not to be any more casualties, or fatalities, for that matter.'

'Yeah.'

'Okay,' Buckley continued. 'Now, Caroline, do you think you could maybe tell me what's brought this all on?'

'Andrew McNally.'

'Could you tell me who that is?'

Caroline looked at the floor.

Samuel sat down against the wall, as best as he could without the cable tie digging into his wrist.

'Tell me about McNally, Caroline,' he began. 'What did he do to shit all over your parade?'

Caroline didn't answer.

'You've got the entire bloody police and media circus out there,' Samuel continued. 'More so the police, which is what you wanted, isn't it? Why'd you bring the gun, if you never intended to hurt anyone?'

Eventually, Caroline also sat down, still holding her gun. Momentarily, she looked at the gun as though it had been an afterthought. She leaned against the wall adjacent to the door. Did she have a family? A partner - husband, wife? Young or adult children? Potentially devastated family because Caroline would never come home? Would they have been watching as this situation unfolded on the news, or worse still, have been among the crowd on the other side of the door? Wondering why she was doing it - what thoughts were racing around in that mind of hers? Pleading for Caroline to do the right thing - hand herself in, without injury, and end this. Of course, that was what Samuel wanted. Maybe Caroline's family didn't give a rat's arse. Rot in hell, you bitch, that sort of thing. Drifted or completely estranged - the opposite of Joan, who didn't seem to be let out of her brother's sight. How much of her own life did she live, that she had come to Samuel in the first place? He was still asking himself that same question, despite how long her therapy had been going on for. You may not have been able to choose your family, but Joan deserved better. Better than Samuel. Someone who didn't test the patience of every poor soul they encountered. Who got it wrong about people more than they would have liked?

Samuel certainly didn't want to start assuming things about Caroline - this job had mostly buried that hatchet long ago. He had heard it all from his many clients over the years, but maybe he hadn't. His, Caroline's, and everyone on the other side's lives were hanging on the line - there was no word for how that felt. Being held by a woman with a gun in this toilet - had Samuel fucked up one time too many? Oh, he just wanted to call Harriet again - hug her, tell her this would all be over soon. Not for the next time she saw him to be her treating him in the ICU - or worse, in a body bag. Nor Joan. He didn't want that to the fate of the woman sitting by the door, nursing her gun. The sooner he knew about Andrew McNally, the better.

'Caroline,' Samuel began, treading ever carefully on his words. 'I'd like to leave here at some point, preferably alive and back home, and I imagine everyone out there would too. How about we talk - or you talk, and maybe I - Buckley and I - can try to help you?'

'Caroline? Samuel?'

'Yeah?' Samuel called.

'What happening in there, are you all right?'

Samuel glanced between Caroline and the door.

'Caroline's going to talk to me! Tell me what's wrong!'

Why couldn't she just tell Buckley, and get this over with?

'All right,' Buckley replied. 'But Caroline...we've armed police standing by. Please don't make us use them.'

Caroline didn't answer. Samuel looked at her. Was she-

'You'll be listening as well, then?'

'Yes, Caroline.'

She paused, considering, and then nodded.

'Right.'

Samuel kept his eyes trained on her, every second passing slower than the last. He rather doubted that Buckley and everyone else out were okay with it, but none of them had a choice.

'How is your relationship with your wife?'

Samuel blinked. His relat... His relationship? His relationship with his wife? He looked Caroline over several times, her question...just...beginning...to register.

'It's fine.'

She began to run her hand over the barrel of her gun.

'A wife at your own will?'
'Yes.'

'How long?'

'Twenty years.'

The rubbing stopped.

'Was she the first? First love, I mean?'

In what way was this relevant? What way appropriate?

Samuel shook his head.

'Third.'

He was still treading quite carefully. Harriet would not likely appreciate having the ins and outs of their marriage divulged to a complete stranger. Except Caroline wasn't a stranger - or certainly she wasn't going to be by the end of all this.

'And you always knew you liked women?'

'Yes.'

Caroline sat back against the wall.

'McNally would have liked you - as a client, I mean.

'Yeah?'

Silence.

'I never even mentioned it. "Oh, but you are".'

There was a level of disgust in that last sentence, which Samuel hadn't noticed before.

'It was my hair,' Caroline continued. 'Never mind my clothes, it must have been my hair.'

'What were you there for, originally?'

Caroline didn't respond for a few minutes.

'Depression. Trouble with my parents.'

The second bit was a little more hesitant - some sort of pain that was buried deep.

'And McNally just brought up your appearance himself one day, you didn't...'

'"There's a woman I know, who'd be just the ticket for you. She's free Friday night".'

Samuel could see where this was heading.

'I couldn't...' Caroline continued, her voice beginning to break. 'My parents, they couldn't...they couldn't find out.'

She didn't seem to notice the watery mass filling her eyes. Samuel watched warily, as Caroline squeezed her hand tightly around the barrel, sniffling.

'And then that I lied about it in the first place...'

Samuel paused, taking in every consideration as to how to respond.

'Did you go?'

Caroline inhaled, wiping her nose, and rubbing her red-rimmed eyes.

'I...I co...'

She nodded, bit by bit.

'What did your parents think?'

Six

July 1996

Caroline had done it, and that was all that mattered. Muriel had been a nice woman. Understanding, when Caroline had apologised for needing to leave early - even offering the taxi fare or a lift home. Muriel didn't once mention McNally, so neither did Caroline. She couldn't. He might have been watching them from two tables behind, for all she knew. The date was done, all down to a tee - even a kiss on the lips. Caroline wouldn't have to brace herself for the sight - even the voice - of her parents. Thank Christ. They would never accept her uttering the Lord's name in vain within earshot, let alone this. It was a man she'd seen tonight, as far as they knew. Mum had made her and Dad's thoughts on Caroline's cropped hairstyle clear ten years ago. "That was some dare your mates gave you".Maybe that was just expected for people of their age - their generation. Just maybe, stepping into that man's office again on Monday would be a little easier now. McNally was a rather scrawny man, a little taller than Caroline, yet had something...something that stopped you being able to tell him "no". Not charisma, but something.

Caroline unlocked the front door. Nine o'clock. They'd appreciate her early return, at least. The door shut behind her, as she entered the hallway. The television sounded from the living room.

'Caroline?'

Mum appeared in the kitchen doorway, arms folded. Her curly bob framed her fierce scowl. Wrapped in her evening attire of a pink silk dressing gown and slippers.

'Maurice, she's here.'

Dad emerged from the living room, appearing not to have changed from his work clothes, looking set to pull the last of his thin, balding hair out.

'You know my blood pressure's been to hell and back this last while,' he began. 'Of all the things to hide...how many other women before this one tonight?'

Caroline froze.

No.

'I-I'm not. I've never-'

'Enough.'

Caroline's eyes darted between her parents. Somewhere in her mind, she could see Andrew McNally's face just...see him and Muriel celebrating.

'Dad, I never-'

He continued, his voice quiet and calm, a rage simmering on its edge.

'No grandchildren - legitimate grandchildren. Did you even think about that?'

Caroline bit her trembling lip. Fought to stop her tears. She'd never thought about them, ever. Caroline couldn't turn away from her mum's silent stony glare. Her voice had caught in her throat. Nothing she said would...

Dad's stare was set.

'I'll be talking with Mr McNally again in the morning.'

Caroline watched him retreat into the living room.

Eventually Mum returned into the kitchen, arms still folded. Caroline was in two minds about whether to follow her. She exhaled...then did.

Mum had started preparing a cup of tea.

'Mum, please let me explain.'

No response, other than the boiling kettle. Dad's anger could never compare to Mum's silence.

'When did he call you and Dad?'
Still no answer.

'Did he come here? Please, Mum, just talk to me.'

Nothing.

Maybe she could try Dad again. Caroline headed for the living room, and stood in the doorway. Maybe he...

Dad's chair was empty. The television was blaring away. She glanced around, then felt something move against the back of the door.

'Dad!'

Caroline rushed to the man slumped between the wall and door, panic clouding her sight of his pale face.

'Mum! Mum, it's Dad!'

She heard Mum's footsteps rush in.

'What is-'

A horrid cry sounded.

Caroline shot up and out to the landline, hearing every bit of her mum's frantic voice.

'Maurice! Maurice! Oh God, Caroline, I think he's had a heart attack!'

Caroline's breathing became rapid, as she held the receiver to her ear.

'*Emergency, which service?*'

'Ambulance, ple-

'Caroline, he's stone cold!'

She heaved out a long, laboured breath.

'My dad...he's just died.'

Seven

'I was twenty-three. What good was living doing me?'

Caroline's head was buried in her arms. She couldn't stop the tears. The pained, pained tears. Samuel looked to the door, hoping Buckley had been listening - that he could help Caroline. Perhaps he and Samuel had been helping all this time, simply by listening. Samuel couldn't remember the last time he had dealt with a suicidal client. He did remember the day Harriet had to deal with eight casualties from a train wreck, and that the remains of both the woman and her car had to be pried off from the entire front of the train. That was just another day for her. A day that could be forgotten in twenty years. That wouldn't matter eventually. Never to Andrew McNally, anyway. This was a day was that going matter. To Samuel. To Caroline. To Harriet. To Joan - all of his clients, in fact. To everyone on the other side of that door.

Samuel longed to talk to Harriet again, as much as she probably did, even if it was only for a minute. The panic - the uncertainty - in her voice was rattling around horribly in his mind. Not as much as his fear of never hearing Harriet's voice - or seeing her again, though. She was a patient woman - she'd wait until Oasis reunited, for Christ's sake - but this was indubitably going to be the ultimate test.

With suicidal clients, in a normal situation, Samuel would have to break confidentiality with the appropriate people. In a normal situation, and...if Caroline was a client. Andrew McNally had been right about one thing. Caroline did need help - though if anything, his idea of help would not have been worth entertaining. Did McNally become a therapist simply to prey on vulnerable people? Samuel shuddered. There were no adjectives for McNally to justify the fact that Caroline had come to this, whatever it was. Enjoying the finer things in life in a lavish house, all at the expense of people who had more baggage than they could cope with. Everyone had their demons. McNally drip-fed every last fibre of his into his patients (they definitely were *not* his clients), and left them to die at the side of the road. Probably got off on it too, the dirty...

Samuel could empathise with Caroline, having lost his mother to cancer when he was six years-old. Perhaps he ought to share this with the distraught woman opposite him. Would it help, as it had done with some of his clients? Joan had seemed to find a certain comfort from his occasional accounts of his school days. When Billy Shepherd dumped a load of PVA glue on his hair. Or, amidst one of the worst winters on record, Rhea Gilliam's stinging balls of ice pounding against the back of his neck, leading to an awful spell of hypothermia. Mr Glover's nonchalant 'don't be such an attention whore' remark. Their laughter still rang like tinnitus. Samuel recalled that Joan had been comforted by his sentiment that she wasn't alone. Week by week, that lovely smile of hers had gradually shone through. A smile that that tyrant brother of hers would never welcome. Joan was a broken lady, but thank Christ she had been able to see the light she had so greatly deserved. She'd probably find comfort just hearing his voice on the phone at this time, as much as Harriet would. You aren't alone. That's what Samuel wanted to tell Caroline; tell his fourteen year-old self all those years ago - but the latter wasn't important right now. Oh, Caroline. What was she going to do? Or not do?

'Did he do anything else, Caroline?'

Silence.

'It would be helpful, for the police at least, to know.'

Caroline cradled back and forth, seemingly lost - detached, even.

Samuel remembered the interaction he'd had with Joan's brother Peter about the exceptions of client confidentiality - McNally was a therapist, after all.

'I'm sorry to have to even ask this, Caroline,' Samuel continued. 'But was there any...sexual abuse? Or physical?'

Caroline stopped, staring at the floor. She seemed to have forgotten all about the gun.

'"I don't care how many girls you did it with",' Caroline began quietly. 'Mum's last words to me. Four days before I was just about able to identify her on the carriage windscreen.'

No. That train wreck. It couldn't...no. Bloody hell.

'"How are we today, Carol?"'

Her voice began to rise, utter contempt spilling through. Samuel looked as Caroline squeezed her hand around the barrel of the gun, again.

'"How was your weekend?"'

Her breathing - her voice - they were beginning to escalate, as if she was having a panic attack.

'"How was-"'

Caroline shot up.

Samuel watched as she bound past him towards the sinks.

'Caroline!'

She dropped the gun in one of the sinks, and began to pace between the sinks and the urinal. No point in trying to move, not with this cable tie digging into Samuel's wrist.

'Caroline,' he began, keeping his voice low and measured. 'Caroline, please don't-'

'Don't what?'

Caroline's voice was also low, but the panic had resurfaced. Or was it just simply frustration? Samuel had an inkling of how she wanted to finish that question. Don't blame yourself for your father's death. Or any of the other things. How he wanted to tell her that.

Taking in every bit of the frenzied state of the woman before him, he had to tread carefully.

'Caroline...if you start tearing it up in here, that lot'll be in faster than *Wile E. Coyote.*'

Caroline paced and paced, never once catching Samuel's gaze.

'I don't imagine Buckley wants that any more than us. I certainly don't.'

He spoke to no effect - and instead Caroline continued to pace up and down, though probably not as fast as the thoughts running through her mind.

She bound across to Samuel, hauling him up.

"Big Aunty Siobhan wouldn't be doing too many cartwheels about you sleeping with little cousin Lorraine, I bet".

She spat out each word with every bit of anger - abhorrence - she could muster. Samuel could see everything in her eyes. Torment. Guilt. Frustration. A lost soul deprived of so much. A wound that had never stopped bleeding. None of which she deserved.

"Progress is always in us therapists' best interests and intentions. If that progress were to be hindered..."

Caroline let go and approached the toilet door, leaning towards the bullet holes.

'Dirty little fucker - I'm a dirty little fucker.'

'Are you all right, Caroline?' Buckley called. 'What about Samuel, is-

'I'm fine, yeah!'

'Okay.'

The biggest lie Samuel would ever tell. All for Caroline's sake. It wasn't going to do any favours, not in the long run. It was what would unravel this whole thing. Put both of them on their deathbeds. The lie that Harriet would never forgive him for. All for a woman he had never met before...half an hour ago.

'Dirty little fu...How many officers are actually out there?'

Samuel glanced between Caroline and the door.

'Why do you want to know that, Caroline?' Buckley finally answered.

'How many?'
'There are six armed officers, Caroline.'

Yes, why did she want to know that? Not that Samuel couldn't guess. Caroline moved away, heading towards the sinks, and picked up her gun.

'Put it down, but why should I? Why should I, Andrew?'

She started towards Samuel.

'You and your bastarding white hair.'

Caroline aimed the gun straight at his face. Samuel made to move, raising his hands, and-

Damn this cable tie.

'Carol-'

'*What*, Andrew - *what*, Andrew - WHAT, Andrew?!'

Her face was set, red as a bad sunburn.

'What's going on in there? Caroline? Samuel?'

Samuel glanced between Caroline and the door.

'Nothing, I'm just trying to keep her calm!'

Bloody hell, another lie - why, Samuel, you...

'Are you trying to put me out of a job?'

Of course not. Buckley was the one equipped to deal with people like Caroline. Well, hostages like Caroline. People - clients - like her had come and gone through Samuel's office over the last twelve years, like the rain and sun.

'No! I-I'm sorry, no!'

'Okay,' Buckley called. 'How is she?'

Samuel looked at Caroline. At the barrel aimed at his face. If Buckley broke down that door, he'd see. Or would he? Caroline was just another inconvenience for that lot outside, who Buckley was pretending to care about, wasn't she? Caroline hadn't even had that; someone pretending to care. A sick, predatory, pathetic excuse for a human being. With all the rotten week-old trimmings. With his eyes so focused on Caroline and the gun - but mainly Caroline - he realised he had left Buckley hanging. And blown whatever cover he'd barely convinced himself he had made. Though probably none at all, if Buckley had been listening all along.

'Caroline?' Buckley called. 'I'd like to talk to you. Do you think...we could do that?'

His voice was soft, laced with sympathetic undertones, which Samuel was all too familiar with. The superficial type which could be about as useful as reverse psychology, at times.

'Why don't you, Caroline?' Samuel said, keeping his eyes off the gun as best he could, but still approaching it like stepping stones. 'Maybe it...will help.'

Caroline was keeping herself prisoner in this toilet, the way McNally had done to her mind all those years ago. The former seemed to have been by choice, the latter not so much.

She stared at Samuel, and then the gun. Bit by bit, she lowered it.

'But Andrew wants to help, he says I need help...'

'Which Buckley may be able to give you...over at the door.'

Stepping stones, Samuel, stepping stones.

'Caroline,' Buckley called. 'I've been listening, and understand what you've told

Samuel. But I'd like, now, to try and get you both out of there, as safely as possible.'

Caroline's hand trembled, and she looked as though she would start crying again.

'Andrew isn't here,' Samuel said, trying that same soft and sympathetic voice Buckley had used. 'It's just the three of us. No A...we won't use his name, how about that?'

Caroline sniffed, her hand now frantically shaking.

'Do you think you could do that - g-go over and talk with Buckley - for me?'

The shaking became trembling, then nothing, and the gun fell out of her hand, and Samuel caught it - as best he could with one free hand. Caroline wandered towards the door, and eventually sat down next to it.

'I'm here.'

'Do you still have the gun, Caroline?'

She shook her head, looking at Samuel.

'Andrew has it.'

'Do you mean Samuel, Caroline?'

'He's got the gun.'

'But Samuel's not going to use it, is he?'

Caroline's tears were choking up in her throat.

'I...Why doesn't he? Just finish...'

'I don't imagine Samuel has much of a desire to hurt you, Caroline,' Buckley replied, to which Samuel shook his head in response. 'I would certainly hope not.'

She heaved a huge sniff, leaning her head back against the wall.

'I ran so far. But I didn't.'

'What do you mean, Caroline?' Buckley asked.

Caroline looked to Samuel.

'You wouldn't let me, Andrew,' she spat. 'And now you won't finish it.'

Samuel held tightly onto the gun.

'I am not letting you have this,' he began. 'An - he's not here, Caroline. He can't, and won't hurt you, any more than what he has. Buckley and I only want to help you - I swear. Please, please, try and understand that.'

Caroline continued to heave out huge sniffs, with the odd sob. Had she heard any of that? Samuel bloody hoped so.

'Samuel's right, Caroline,' Buckley called. 'We only want to help, nothing more. But...your question about the number of armed officers...that, uh...that was quite concerning to me. I just-'

'But not to Andrew, it's what he wants. I ran so far.'

Samuel set the gun aside. He didn't know what Caroline meant by that, and was beginning to think she didn't either.

'Ran where, Caroline?'

Eight

12.9.88

Well diary, it happened again. In what is only my third entry, I have to tell you this again. Derek ran starkers through Mrs Landon's cabbage patch for the second Monday running, and Laura's not made much ground in her bikini waxing course. Church was boring as ever yesterday, though not as boring as Mr Reed's algebra. Mum still thinks I'm the one who broke the vase in the hall on Friday - it was Dad, but he's having none of it, 'cause apparently a bottle and a half of scotch doesn't count. D's birthday next week, should be good. Been teasing him about getting to open up his work in the mornings now, we have, but he's chuffed, bless him. It'll be lovely. L said if the bikini waxing doesn't work out, she'd still like to try joining the 'nunion', as she calls it, having recently been cast as a nun in the school's The Sound of Music *production. Have to stay behind for English revision workshop for* Of Mice and Men *questions - Miss Atkinson's pushing me to do higher tier. Suppose it'll be worth it, if I want to be in her shoes one day. In the meantime, gonna see if the local newsagent's looking any workers. Maybe it'll stop my parents harping on and on, God's sake (they won't see this, so no 'lord's name in vain' lecture, thank fudge). Sometimes I'm glad I don't have any siblings, no unnecessary sharing for a start. I'd get the blame (as always), and big Tommy two-shoes would walk scot-free. Wouldn't be called Tommy, actually - it'd be Leonard, or Prudence, if it was a sister. Be back later, diary.*

Benny Nielsen in the sixth form reckons with all the teachers going on maternity leave, the bets for who out-shags who are riding high enough for early retirement - Ms Carneal's onto a winner there. Lamb, mash, and carrots for tea - still better than the muck they call school dinners. Egg/onion or tuna sandwiches, or stew, or a roll with something that wouldn't pass for chicken in this house. Hope Lenny gets to tend his rabbits, for he sure bloody loves them that much. Curley'll probably put paid to that. D said he doesn't want anything special for his BD, so I'll get him some comics - not that reading will stop any more of his antics (Mrs L's surely sick of his mum's apologies by now). Maybe it will stop Big Mandy in the year below calling him 'Del Boy Spaz', faggot, or shirt-lifter. He can't help who he fancies, hell, no one can, so thanks a fucking bunch, Thatcher. Still wants to go into construction when he leaves school, but I reckon Mr Ali will keep him on in the local. Just remembered that Shaun

Gooders had an erection in Science during an experiment, which Bryson handed him three days suspension for. Doris Michael later told me it must've been one wet dream about Debbie Harry too many - boys and their toys.

Nine

'Is this a dagger which I see before me, the handle toward my hand? Come, let me clutch thee.'

Moylan looked not at his page, but whimsically at George Osmond, as the student read aloud from his book. That sumptuous strawberry blonde hair. You weren't supposed to have favourites in this profession, but so what? For fifteen years, Moylan had had his favourites. These boys were all so fresh, and innocent, they wouldn't know any better. How serendipitous that George was in need of Moylan's after school workshop today. George Osmond and a few others. Harvey McDowell. Ritchie Keenan. Lewis Sanford. Oh, yes.

The school bell sounded.

Moylan stood up, approaching the blackboard.

'Very good, thank you, George.'

He lifted a fresh piece of chalk, peering brightly over his twenty lads.

'We shall finish that act tomorrow,' he said, eyeing Lewis Sanford. 'In the meantime, finish your notes for Thursday's lesson. I hope to see more of you at today's workshop.'

Not a word was uttered, instead some merely nodded.

'Off you go.'

The class finally arose, pushing in chairs and packing away books and stationary into their school bags. They began to file out in an orderly fashion, just as it should have been.

'Oh, Ritchie, could I...?' Moylan called, smiling at the boy sporting a blonde crew cut.

Ritchie Keenan made his way over to Moylan, who watched as the door finally shut. Keenan was just the right size. The right build.

'Nothing too terrible, Ritchie. Just regarding the workshop this afternoon...'

Moylan brought his mug of coffee up to his mouth, taking several long sips. Five-thirty. This afternoon had been wonderfully productive. Oh, yes. Brian Scanlon and Helen Turner had been engaged in some tedious discussion about window glazing, for the last three-quarters of an hour - almost twice the time Moylan had spent nursing his beverage. Helen was clearly growing sick of it, but politely engaged until Brian finally shut up. Moylan smiled. At least the conversation during the lift home, that Helen had gratefully accepted, would cleanse her palate.

'Won't be too long, Peter,' Helen called, heading to the table. 'Just going to sort my belongings.'

Moylan flashed a smile. Dear, oh dear, what was that scowl across Brian's face all about? Brian came over next to Moylan, rinsing out his mug. He set it aside, and looked straight at Moylan.

'Enjoying it, are you?'

Moylan didn't even glance at his now-lukewarm coffee.

'Well, a day like today, one needs perking up.'

Brian's stare didn't ease up, and he heaved out a long sigh.

'My brother never had his first beer, and the blinding hangover the next morning,' he began. 'The keys to his first house. His first heartbreak. The... None of that means a thing to people like you, of course.'

Moylan let a slight smirk creep out.

'Well, as an only child, I'd imagine not.

Brian's face was turning red as lobster. Such unnecessary anger.

'Fourteen years-old, Moylan. Fo-'

'And barely wiping the drool from his chin, yes? The ways of the world watered down - sugar-coated - for him, until the elder sibling decides it's deep enough to throw him in? Dear, oh, dear, what a loss, indeed.'

Brian paused, utterly seething. He stepped back, scoffing.

'Trying to fuck Helen up as much as you've been doing to Ritchie Keenan,' he said quietly. 'At least they have people who love them.'

Two could play at this game - Brian's default strategy. And a bit tiring. Moylan gave him a warm smile.

'Above the waist is usually ideal, Brian.'

Moylan moved away, just as Helen emerged clutching a bag and several files.

'Ready, my dear? Let's go.'

Ten

Samuel looked at the woman sitting by the door, letting out loud sobs occasionally. Buckley had been trying his best with Caroline.

'I'm not...oh, there's no point, no...'

It was Samuel's turn now. His turn to not fuck this up.

'What happened next, Caroline?'

Caroline looked at him, still detached. Still distant.

'Did you get to do your A levels? Or Laura and Derek, what happened to them?'

She brought her hand to her mouth.

'Don't want to talk about it,' she said almost inaudibly.

Samuel nodded, hopefully showing Caroline that he understood.

He had encountered many like Caroline over the last twelve years, so why did something seem different about her? No, not different. 'Different' was the whole reason people wound up in therapy - why it existed in the first place. In a way, one 'different' too many could've been seen as the root of the world's evils - the building blocks for this profession, if you will. A backhanded way of saying 'strange', or 'weird'. Or in Jude Biggerstaff's case...spa...

No. Samuel couldn't even bring himself to finish the word, that horrible word. That Caroline's friend Derek had been called. Someone would dare say it was different times, but that didn't mean it was okay, though, did it?

Caroline only seemed 'different' because Samuel was thinking under duress - that was it, wasn't it? If anyone was 'different', it was Jude. Not that Samuel had ever seen Jude that way. Oh, lovely Jude.

Buckley began to talk with Caroline again, but their voices seemed to fading out. Samuel was watching Caroline, but thinking of Jude.

Eleven

Forrest Gump was right, life was like a box of chocolates. It lobbed the complete unrelenting set of hardback books at you with all the subtlety of a cold shower, and then some. Certainly Samuel's mother's death twelve years ago had for him. The big C. That's all he was ever told, until he turned sixteen two years ago. His father's rubbing of the back of his neck when asked about it said it all to Samuel. Forty-one years old his mother was, but had never looked a day over thirty-five. She didn't smoke, and her side of the family all lived to around eighty. A mystery to everyone else, particularly his mother's sister, who had taken to dusting her knick-knacks and washing her kitchen walls till she could give Dr Nick Riviera's grease-soaked paper a run for its money. The house had been the epitome of a loving-and-caring kind of lifestyle. It must have been gnawing bit-by-bit at his mother for years, just waiting for the right moment. Surprisingly, no one in school had teased Samuel about his loss, in fact, more recently hadn't gone near him. Not even during his free periods in the library. Most of his mates were based in his neighbourhood. Hadn't seen them in a couple of days, though, not even Jude. Life was a box of chocolates; death was a hornets' nest that a child's parents forbade it to kick.

Samuel sat at his desk placed adjacent to his bed, looking at the paper spread across it, combing his fingers through his long locks. He had a deadline for Monday, and groaned at the thought of doing nothing but slaving over this seven-hundred word essay for Psychology. It was probably the strongest of his three subjects, in terms of what he could do with it after school. Samuel rubbed his eyes, and rose from the desk. He surveyed his bomb site of a bedroom, particularly at the crumpled heap of shirts and socks stuffed in the corner, and the numerous empty glasses decorating his chest of drawers. At some point, his father would have to tell him to wise up, but it would probably never come. Not if his father's shifts at the train station were anything to go by. How many more nights of pasta could Samuel stomach, he wondered. His father didn't bother with any of it - had his head buried in a book, or ears on the sports on the radio, when he had time. If any of Samuel's mates turned up at the house, his father pretty much shrugged it off "as long as they weren't gonna choke up their lungs full of Marlboro's".

One of these weekends, maybe Samuel and Jude could go to the pictures. Or take a venture to Blockbusters and rent Jude's all-time favourite, *Stand By Me*, for the thousandth time. Either that, or seeing where she stood on Rick Deckard being a replicant or not.

At this rate, it would have to be summer, when everything was done and dusted and Samuel would be free - well, for a couple of months, anyway. University, or some similar endeavour was awaiting. It would be if he did just wise-up a bit. He did cherish what could have been considered an incentive from Jude's mother, Cynthia.

"You've got brains to burn, Samuel. Doing Ruby proud, just as you are for me and Jude".

Maybe he should pay Jude a visit over the weekend.

Samuel sat near the front of the half-empty bus, as it rode along. It was a half-hour journey to Jude's, but worth it. More so, now that summer had finally arrived - even if it had done nothing but rain. Never bothered Samuel though, or Jude, for that matter. Jude would splash in the puddles all day, if given free rein. Her shiny new red and blue wellingtons would make her the talk of the town - or would at least suffice as a distraction from the pot plants Cynthia had created from the old ones. The bus came to the next stop, and a man stepped on. Wearing his usual black overcoat, to match his coffee-tone skin. He paid his fare and took a seat near the back, hands resting on his thighs. Then it started. The man's temples throbbed - breathed in and out, as if with a mind of their own. Still as unnerving as when Samuel first noticed it however long ago, amazingly. He knew, even at his age, to only ever be Throbbing Temples' captive audience discreetly, but Jude...well, it would be with the same awe and fascination she had with Linda Blair's spinning head in *The Exorcist*, that she'd watch. Jude didn't mean to cause the scenes she did at times. Cynthia made that crystal clear to the ones who dared to open that can of worms, and rightly so.

Samuel rang the bell, as the bus gradually arrived at his stop. He alighted, quickly glancing at Throbbing Temples, as the bus moved on. None the wiser, it seemed. Just a five minute walk, and Samuel would be finally be at the Biggerstaff household.

Samuel pushed open the front gate of the semi-detached bungalow. The area Jude and Cynthia resided in was decent enough. The neighbours, too. Apart from the odd few. If the gift-wrapped turd and complimentary "Hey Jude, the spazzy prude" note through the Biggerstaff's letterbox last week were anything to go by.

A woman from two doors appeared. Ursula Olsen. The woman Cynthia had suspected as the culprit of it, and numerous other repulsive assaults on the Biggerstaff's home. The front windows smeared with rotting cheese and eggs. Maggots falling down the chimney into the living room. All conveniently at night or in the early hours, too. The police couldn't do anything, because there'd been no proof it was Olsen. Olsen would have egged on some of the other more impressionable youths from the next street, if ever she was caught doing the dirty deed herself. Samuel thought worse things would have been getting the thin middle-aged woman's goat. Did divorce really affect people that badly? Mr Olsen had taken his half of the wardrobe, his teapot, and typewriter, and buggered off like merry hell. That was all Samuel knew. Word had it that Mr Olsen now resided in his second of three homes in Bulgaria, thanks to all those mad business endeavours he'd finally had the luck of the draw with.

'Veery wie mates's o' yurs.'

Samuel stopped, looking at Olsen, habitually wincing at the thick accent, as if still hearing it for the first time.

'Sorry?'

'Doin' the dirty on yuh once they foun' ou' the retard escap'd from the loony bin.'

Samuel rolled his eyes, and moved on. Not this again. As he started down the path, he looked to see Cynthia in the front window. A friendly face, at last. Cynthia had her trademark pink cardigan and polka dot dress draped over her busty figure, along with her cream slippers. Still looking good for fifty-three. Cynthia smiled as radiantly as her golden locks, and they exchanged a wave, as Samuel approached the front door.

Some moments later, Cynthia answered.

'All right, Samuel?' she chirped, widening the door. 'Come on through.'

Samuel entered, and Cynthia shut it behind them. 'Jude! Samuel's here!'

A sprightly, slim young woman appeared from the kitchen doorway, grasping a snooker cue. Good to see Jude's slightly messy sandy hair hadn't changed. Nor her favourite shirt, the blue one with elephants.

'Oh, Jude, go put your shorts on,' Cynthia said softly, and only then did Samuel notice Jude's bare legs and feet. 'I don't fancy scrubbing your lunch off them afterwards, eh?'

Cynthia's tone had been typically gentle, as she didn't feel harshness was the way to go with her daughter, even if Jude could be a handful at times. There was something about that which Samuel liked. Of course, it may have been different behind closed doors, though it seemed unlikely.

Jude grinned, letting out a little squeal, and bound past them to the stairs.

'Oi, oi, Jude,' Cynthia called, reaching out her arm. 'Give that here while you're up there. Don't want any accidents, do we?'

Never breaking her smile, Jude passed her the cue and disappeared up the stairs.

'Just you go on into the living room, Samuel. I'll get you some water.'

Samuel thanked her and headed into the living room.

The warm cream finish certainly looked as if it was certainly lived in. Some clothes were strewn over the grey sofa in the corner, as well as some slippers on the red carpet. Were probably all Jude's. A few framed photos of Cynthia and Jude were proudly displayed along the fireplace and table under the living room window. Samuel glanced at his - and Cynthia's, for that matter - favourite, in which a younger Jude beamed as she clutched a well-deserved snooker trophy. it was things like this which almost made Cynthia forget vermin like Olsen existed in the world. That lovely smile of Jude's, it was just simply a part of her - epitomised her personality, so to speak. The sunshine in Cynthia's life, since her husband had vanished many years ago. Went for a packet of cigarettes one morning, and just disappeared. Cynthia had confided the warts-and-all details to Samuel one spring morning, keeping Jude preoccupied with *Fireman Sam* video tapes. Cynthia's anguish, grief - even her depression - it wasn't a matter of empathy for Samuel. It was far beyond that. He tried his best with the right way to tell her this. To not fuck up such a moment. Cynthia's subsequent desire to share a hug with him proved his move had indeed been a wise one.

Samuel sat down on the sofa, removing his shoes - he was the guest, after all. More like a family member. The brother Jude never had - the son Cynthia never had. Or was Cynthia the mother Samuel had hardly had? What a shame you couldn't choose your family.

'Here you are,' Cynthia said, entering with Samuel's glass of water and passing it to him. She sat in the armchair beside the window. Samuel always enjoyed their chats, though no doubt the three of them would be immersed in the television before long. It was mainly Jude's call, with the likes of *Dennis and Gnasher*, repeats of *Danger Mouse*, or *'Allo 'Allo* in the evenings. Cynthia had, however, forbidden Jude to watch *Top of the Pops*, because of a slight overexcitement for The Spice Girls.

'We're going out on Thursday, you ought to come along. Just into town - get Jude away from the telly for a bit, you know?'

Thumping could be heard from upstairs. Sounded like Jude was having her own little adventure.

'Sure, Samuel nodded, though surprised, despite that this wasn't an uncommon affair. 'What time?'

'Come round about ten, Jude'll maybe have calmed a bit by then, after her meds, and that.'

Cynthia would never directly say it, but it was probably her treat to Samuel for his 'remarkable exam results'.

'Was that ol' bint Olsen giving you grief? Saw you and her out there, seemed a bit...'

Samuel's shoulders sunk.

'I still can't make her out half the time, to be honest, Cynthia. Wouldn't be ideal for a police report, I know.'

'I want to be like that at times, too - you know, just tune it out. But what kind of mother would I be to Jude, then?'

The thumping from upstairs had become sporadic. Samuel considered Jude lucky, that she could be oblivious to Ursula Olsen's unwarranted abuse.

'No less than the one you have been,' Samuel reassured her. 'and I'm not just saying that.'

'Of course not. You've always been so good to Jude, you know.'

Just being a friend, same as she is to me, was what Samuel wanted to say, but he just smiled modestly.

Thump, thump, thump.

Ah, the lady of the hour.

Jude was now sensibly dressed in her brown shorts, that cheesy grin still plastered across her face.

'Ello, Sammy. Play snooker?'

Cynthia rose.

'Not just yet, Jude,' she said. Lunchtime soon, it'll have to be after that, okay?'

Jude squeaked, clapping.

'Meatballs,' she exclaimed happily. 'Meatballs and 'sketti.'

'No, no, Jude, that's for dinner. Ham sandwiches for lunch.'

'Sammiches.'

Samuel smiled at Jude.

'Oh yeah,' he chirped. 'Your mum makes the best ham sandwiches, doesn't she?'

Jude nodded. 'Yah.'

'Gonna need them to help you beat me at snooker, aren't you?'

Jude nodded excitedly.

Cynthia chuckled as she looked between them, heading for the door.

'You want any, Samuel?'

'Aw no, I can get something at home later, but thank you, of course.'

Cynthia flashed a smile and exited into the kitchen.

Even the crusts of her four triangle ham sandwiches hadn't stood a chance against Jude. She polished them off by picking each individual crumb they had dared to leave behind. Tough choice for this afternoon's entertainment - *Mrs Doubtfire*, *The Goonies*, or a marathon of *Keeping Up Appearances* repeats on BBC Two. Jude had grown rather fond of Robin Williams as of late, but liked that ever misfortunate Bucket woman more.

Jude's reward for absolutely kicking Samuel's snooker-sucking arse three times over. Not until after her daily dish-washing adventure, always under Cynthia's cautious eye, of course. The only task Jude couldn't really do independently was wash herself - which always had to be a bath, as the spraying water from the shower had been akin to Dustin Hoffman's distressed screams towards aeroplane travel in *Rain Man*. That was merely an echo for now, as the three of them chuckled at Hyacinth Bucket's frustrated exchange with yet another Chinese takeaway call.

'Spicy prawn balls!' Jude giggled with delight.

'Don't imagine you'd like those very much, Jude,' Samuel said. 'You'd need several gallons of water after, you would.'

'Not to mention your number twos,' Cynthia added, grimacing playfully.

Jude screwed up her face, sticking out her tongue. 'Yucky, yucky!'

A full day out on Thursday. If only seeking his parents' permission was still a thing. It was an experience that he missed sometimes. Samuel glanced at his watch. Almost four - time to go, sadly.

'Ten o'clock on Thursday, yeah?'

Cynthia also noted the time.

'That you away, then?' Yes, yes, about ten. Jude - Samuel's going now.'

Samuel looked at Jude, who was still glued to the television.

'Going to say goodbye to me, Jude?'

It seemed as if Jude hadn't been listening, but then she turned to him.

'Going now? Sammy going?'

Samuel nodded. 'Do I get a hug before I do?'

He stood up, outstretching his arms. Jude squeaked as she sprung up, and wrapped her arms around him. These hugs were something Samuel always cherished. Jude would probably have hugged you to death, if left to it.

'Okay,' Samuel said at last. 'That's good, that's good, Jude. All right?'

Gradually, with a little nudge from Cynthia, Jude released him.

'You can give me an extra big one on Thursday, eh?'

Jude nodded excitedly, clapping.

'Thursday! Thursday!'

Samuel smiled.

'See you both then.'

Samuel entered the shop across the road from his stop. Still another twenty minutes until his bus home. Steak or salmon for tonight? Harriet was coming over. Two months, but it was surely longer. The most gorgeous woman he'd had the fortune of laying eyes on. Her long red hair complimented just about anything she wore, and made her look notably younger than her true twenty-one years of age. Harriet was an utter brain box, too - her intriguing method of relieving her teenage anger by solving countless quantum equations, always made Samuel chuckle. He couldn't wait to hear how Harriet's training was going - maybe it would prompt him to think about his own career path. Something within the realm of psychology, maybe? It had been his strongest A level, after all. Harriet always seemed keen to hear more about Jude - a genuine interest. Well, she was going to be a nurse. Samuel had debated whether or not to call Harriet before tonight, just to make sure it was all systems go.

Oh, stop worrying yourself, you muppet, she'd call in advance if it wasn't. She always did.

Twelve

'I'd like to hear more about Laura and Derek, Caroline. They sounded like good mates.'

Samuel had said it...subconsciously. Shit. Had he actually...had he *actually* forgotten about Caroline?

No. Surely not. He couldn't forget someone like Caroline.

Buckley - he would have been calling for Samuel, wondering...

Bloody hell. Why had Samuel let himself wander? Wander away with Jude. Let himself neglect his client? Hold on. At what point...

Caroline was beginning to feel like a client. If there was a word for that, like there was Stockholm Syndrome, this was it. Caroline was staring at him. The gun was by her side. Was she too distressed to use it? Or had she forgotten about it?

'What happened to them?'

Caroline shot up over to Samuel, the gun in hand. Samuel froze, alarmed by her speed. Caroline seemed rather alert, as if none of the prior had happened. Samuel couldn't move with those brown eyes set on his. Caroline moved away, and began pacing again.

'Caroline?' Buckley called. 'You okay?'

Caroline paced some more, then stopped.

'Oh, I'm *fineee*, Andrew. But they didn't seem to think so.'

Rather than the quiet, detached tone Caroline had accustomed them to, it was said in an exaggerated southern drawl.

'Who didn't?' Samuel asked. 'Your friends, Laura and Derek?'

Caroline stepped towards the door.

'Six would take me out, wouldn't it?'

Her voice was quiet again. Samuel still had not moved since Caroline had stormed from the door. With his full attention fixed on Caroline, the woman's increasing volatility had firmly stamped out any comforting thoughts of Jude.

Buckley stammered. No doubt, like Samuel, he knew exactly what Caroline meant.

'We really don't want to have to come to that, Caroline. Please f-'

'But they would.'

Caroline moved away from the door. Samuel watched as she approached the urinal.

'Who, Laura and Derek?'

Caroline began to run the gun over the urinal, as if in a way to soothe herself.

'Do you mean him, the one we won't name, Caroline?'

She didn't answer, continuing her soothing action. It was a long shot, but could either Laura or Derek have been among the people outside when Caroline had shot through the door? No. It wasn't a film. It was a terrifying situation that held too many lives on the line, being dictated by a chronically unstable woman. Still with a score to settle? If so, with whom? Andrew McNally? Or, what was beginning to become apparent to Samuel, Caroline herself? Would Samuel ever have the pleasure of acquainting with McNally? He simultaneously hoped so and hoped not.

'Tell me about Laura and Derek. What happened to them?'

Thirteen

5.2.91

Odd day, today, diary. A Chinese woman was banned from the shop for repeatedly shouting 'Bad black man! Bad black man!' at a set of black jazz band figurines. Who knew the Chinese could be racist? Gareth was considering expanding it to all Chinese folk, and had even drafted out the notice. Must be something to do with the chop suey from the takeaway down the road he's still trying to clear his bowels of.

The Fortescue's buried their dog Cupcake this morning. Contrary to the name, it wasn't sweet or tasty, though the Chinese woman would probably disagree. D's going deaf - if it's true that dependence on crisps and shite can cause blindness, it's just as well it ain't that, for I know no one who can teach him Braille. He was apparently just sitting in Maths and started complaining he couldn't hear.

Someone (loudly and deliberately) farted during Billy Bibbit's suicide in English. Wonder what Nurse Ratched would think. Miss Ingram clearly misjudged that A-grade standard work and emotional maturity will never be mutually exclusive.

L offered to go see Dances With Wolves *at the weekend, as a break. Got too much coursework. Pat Goss and a couple of others in my year are planning some sort of end-of-year prank on the teachers. Hopefully Glover will be on his funny half hour.*

Parent's anniversary tomorrow. Expensive meal at that Indian Gareth claims to serve 'little chunks of rotted bark passed off as lamb medallions'. Tried to persuade them towards the Italian three streets away, but nope. They've also arranged cousin Margot to babysit, despite that I will only have McMurphy and Nurse Ratched for company. Might take L up on her offer. Bugger knows what time they'll decide to return - in time for HIGNFY, probably, which Merton and Hislop make unmissable, apparently.

Spent too long listening to Sound of Silence *earlier. Worrying a bit about the extent of Pat Goss's prank. Has he seen* Carrie?

D has actually mulled over the possibility of him also going blind. Not likely with all his sprinting, Weetabix, and longing for the buttocks of the boy from the next cul-de-sac. The would-be BF is called Arnold, but is a coeliac, lives in a bungalow, and only walks twenty minutes to the corner shop for his mother's lotto ticket twice a week, as exercise. So 'The Terminator' *isn't likely to catch on, then. Love is a fucking peculiar thing.*

Will my parents drive to the restaurant, or take a taxi? If it's the former, who'll be designated driver? Neither have been behind the wheel for a good while, so I'm longing for the taxi. They'll be bad Christians and drink too much - but it'll be their night, so why not? If Dad takes his tablets, then what's the worst?

Four hundred more words to go on H&SC assignment. Will ask L about the DWW showtimes. We could always wait a few months and see that new Jodie Foster one, Silence of the Lambs. *Big queues for both? Might try and get her round tomorrow night, or just phone her landline. Well, when she finally escapes from all that oil and grease in Sonny's for the evening. L should ask him for a raise, or better yet, Major for minimum wage. A bottomless pit for bombs and the military, but a shrug of indifference for those practically doing slave labour. L had thought about protesting, but where would it likely get her, diary? Her parents would probably egg it on - I think they'd bask in the fifteen minutes - the headlines, and all that. L once did an* Adrian Mole *and wore red tights instead of black, and her faux-fur coat instead of her blazer, in protest of the uniform rules. Never minded the pinafore, though. Glover's only response: 'Didn't realise Labour were letting birds steer their ship now'. Just wait, Glover, just you wait.*

I can't wait to move away. Get my PGCE. Be an adult, at last. Teach Jane Eyre *and* The Great Gatsby *to other aspiring English intellects. Parents will be glad to see me fly the nest. Dad sees it to be aiming higher than he ever did as a chartered accountant. What's wrong with a CA - he once offered to do the entire street's tax returns, if Thatcher won in '87.*

Awful tired, so will retire for the night. Adios for now, diary.

7.2.91

Persuaded Margot to let me watch my parent's taped Edge of Darkness *episodes, last night. Would it be too much for L? Probably not if she can stomach SOTL. I was only slightly disgusted by the noises from that front door, a little over eight hours ago. Apparently my parents ended up trying to recreate the spaghetti kiss from* Lady and the Tramp *at the Italian (second thoughts about enduring the aftermath of chicken korma, I guess), and Mum's dress got caught in and ripped away by the taxi door. Could still hear her delightful rendition of* 'She'll Be Coming Round The Mountain' *as the milkman did his round.*

L and I have decided on SOTL. Since her bikini-waxing and 'nunion' endeavours went south here is number three: painting portraits at the art college. Won't be surprised if she lobbies for hunk heaven zipped down to the naval.

Seventeen years-old, and I am finally in love. Emmet Griffin, the farmer man's boy. Well, not really, but he does like his plaid shirts and body warmers. Maybe he won't leave the toilet seat up like the rest of the dirty birdies. Two inches shorter than me, which makes a nice change (least I won't have to lend Fergie down the road's laundry basket off her, for all the snogging). Looks like he's trying to go for a George Michael crossed with Jason Donovan look. Suits him. Just as well D has his dream boy, 'cause this boy is so special (to the melody of Brass in Pocke*t, I sang that, diary). First date is next Saturday (you know, coursework the rest of the week, and all that). Emmet's choosing the venue, of course. Letting L meet him tomorrow. Fun times.*

Fourteen

All bad men were cowards. Moylan was a coward. That's what the box before him said. If Brian saw it. If anyone saw it. Moylan wouldn't go down like Warden Norton in *The Shawshank Redemption*.

Everything would end. If Brian Scanlon saw it. Moylan wasn't a coward, but he was. To have a wife had never been a priority. The wife would never forgive him. The wife would ask nagging, incessant questions. The wife wouldn't take his side like she was supposed to. She would hide all the knives from the kitchen that she ought not to.

Moylan stared at the box, one arm on his hip.

A shoe box. They'd be none the wiser. Wouldn't they? He didn't do all that running in the evenings for nothing.

'Those Nikes finally beginning to have seen better days then, eh, Peter?'

Moylan turned his head.

Gavin Woods smiled, a small load of files tucked under his arm.

'Yes.'

How long was Woods going to inconvenience him with wretched small talk?

'You should come with me and the guys on one of our runs some weekend - some practice for sports day, you know?'

Moylan gave a nod.

'I'll think about it.'

Gavin flashed a smile, and turned away. Moylan looked back at the box. Nobody would know.

To be continued…

Printed in Great Britain
by Amazon

64355604R00061